GEORGE MEREDITH

THE GENTLEMAN OF FIFTY AND THE DAMSEL OF NINETEEN

CLEAN BRIGHT CLASSICS

ISBN 978-1974070695 - Paperback edition

17 07 30 01 02

Contents

Chapter 1

He

Passing over Ickleworth Bridge and rounding up the heavily-shadowed river of our narrow valley, I perceived a commotion as of bathers in a certain bright space immediately underneath the vicar's terrace-garden steps. My astonishment was considerable when it became evident to me that the vicar himself was disporting in the water, which, reaching no higher than his waist, disclosed him in the ordinary habiliments of his cloth. I knew my friend to be one of the most absent-minded of men, and my first effort to explain the phenomenon of his appearance there, suggested that he might have walked in, the victim of a fit of abstraction, and that he had not yet fully comprehended his plight; but this idea was dispersed when I beheld the very portly lady, his partner in joy and adversity, standing immersed, and perfectly attired, some short distance nearer to the bank. As I advanced along the bank opposed to them, I was further amazed to hear them discoursing quite equably together, so that it was impossible to say on the face of it whether a catastrophe had occurred, or the great heat of a cloudless summer day had tempted an eccentric couple to seek for coolness in the directest fashion, without absolute disregard to propriety. I made a point of listening for the accentuation of the 'my dear' which was being interchanged, but the key-note to the harmony existing between husband and wife was neither excessively unctuous, nor shrewd, and the connubial shuttlecock was so well kept up on both sides that I chose to await the issue rather than speculate on the origin of this strange exhibition. I therefore, as I could not be accused of an outrage to modesty, permitted myself to maintain what might be invidiously termed a satyr-like watch from behind a forward flinging willow, whose business in life was to look at its image in a brown depth, branches, trunk, and roots. The sole indication of discomfort displayed by the pair was that the lady's hand worked somewhat fretfully to keep her dress from ballooning and puffing out of all proportion round about her person, while the vicar, who stood without his hat, employed a spongy handkerchief from time to time in tempering the ardours of a vertical sun. If you will consent to imagine a bald blackbird, his neck being shrunk in apprehensively, as you may see him in the first rolling of the thunder, you will gather an image of my friend's appearance.

He performed his capital ablutions with many loud 'poofs,' and a casting up of dazzled eyes, an action that gave point to his recital of the invocation of Chryses to Smintheus which brought upon the Greeks disaster and much woe. Between the lines he replied to his wife, whose remarks increased in quantity, and also, as I thought, in emphasis, under the river of verse which he poured forth unbaffled, broadening his chest to the sonorous Greek music in a singular rapture of obliviousness.

A wise man will not squander his laughter if he can help it, but will keep the agitation of it down as long as he may. The simmering of humour sends a lively spirit into the mind, whereas the boiling over is but a prodigal expenditure and the disturbance of a clear current: for the comic element is visible to you in all things, if you do but keep your mind charged with the perception of it, as I have heard a great expounder deliver himself on another subject; and he spoke very truly. So, I continued to look on with the gravity of Nature herself, and I could not but fancy, and with less than our usual wilfulness when we fancy things about Nature's moods, that the Mother of men beheld this scene with half a smile, differently from the simple observation of those cows whisking the flies from their flanks at the edge of the shorn meadow and its aspens, seen beneath the curved roof of a broad oak-branch. Save for this happy upward curve of the branch, we are encompassed by breathless foliage; even the gloom was hot; the little insects that are food for fish tried a flight and fell on the water's surface, as if panting. Here and there, a sullen fish consented to take them, and a circle spread, telling of past excitement.

I had listened to the vicar's Homeric lowing for the space of a minute or so—what some one has called, the great beast-like, bellow-like, roar and roll of the Iliad hexameter: it stopped like a cut cord. One of the numerous daughters of his house appeared in the arch of white cluster-roses on the lower garden-terrace, and with an exclamation, stood petrified at the extraordinary spectacle, and then she laughed outright. I had hitherto resisted, but the young lady's frank and boisterous laughter carried me along, and I too let loose a peal, and discovered myself. The vicar, seeing me, acknowledged a consciousness of his absurd position with a laugh as loud. As for the scapegrace girl, she went off into a run of high-pitched shriekings like twenty woodpeckers, crying: I Mama, mama, you look as if you were in Jordan!'

The vicar cleared his throat admonishingly, for it was apparent that Miss Alice was giving offence to her mother, and I presume he thought it was enough for one of the family to have done so.

'Wilt thou come out of Jordan?' I cried.

'I am sufficiently baptized with the water,' said the helpless man . . .

'Indeed, Mr. Amble,' observed his spouse, 'you can lecture a woman for not making the best of circumstances; I hope you'll bear in mind that it's you who are irreverent. I can endure this no longer. You deserve Mr. Pollingray's ridicule.'

Upon this, I interposed: 'Pray, ma'am, don't imagine that you have anything but sympathy from me.'—but as I was protesting, having my mouth open, the terrible Miss Alice dragged the laughter remorselessly out of me.

They have been trying Frank's new boat, Mr. Pollingray, and they've upset it. Oh! oh' and again there was the woodpeckers' chorus.

'Alice, I desire you instantly to go and fetch John the gardener,' said the angry mother.

'Mama, I can't move; wait a minute, only a minute. John's gone about the geraniums. Oh! don't look so resigned, papa; you'll kill me! Mama, come and take my hand. Oh! oh!'

The young lady put her hands in against her waist and rolled her body like a possessed one.

'Why don't you come in through the boat-house?' she asked when she had mastered her fit.

'Ah!' said the vicar. I beheld him struck by this new thought.

'How utterly absurd you are, Mr. Amble!' exclaimed his wife, 'when you know that the boat-house is locked, and that the boat was lying under the camshot when you persuaded me to step into it.'

Hearing this explanation of the accident, Alice gave way to an ungovernable emotion.

'You see, my dear,' the vicar addressed his wife, she can do nothing; it's useless. If ever patience is counselled to us, it is when accidents befall us, for then, as we are not responsible, we know we are in other hands, and it is our duty to be comparatively passive. Perhaps I may say that in every difficulty, patience is a life-belt. I beg of you to be patient still.'

'Mr. Amble, I shall think you foolish,' said the spouse, with a nod of more than emphasis.

My dear, you have only to decide,' was the meek reply.

By this time, Miss Alice had so far conquered the fiend of laughter that she could venture to summon her mother close up to the bank and extend a rescuing hand. Mrs. Amble waded to within reach, her husband following. Arrangements were made for Alice to pull, and the vicar to push; both in accordance with Mrs. Amble's stipulations, for even in her extremity of helplessness she affected rule and sovereignty. Unhappily, at the decisive moment, I chanced (and I admit it was more than an inadvertence on my part, it was a most ill-considered thing to do) I chanced, I say, to call out—and that I refrained from quoting Voltaire is something in my favour:

'How on earth did you manage to tumble in?'

There can be no contest of opinion that I might have kept my curiosity waiting, and possibly it may be said with some justification that I was the direct cause of my friend's unparalleled behaviour; but could a mortal man guess that in the very act of assisting his wife's return to dry land, and while she was—if I may put it so—modestly in his hands, he would turn about with a quotation that compared him to old Palinurus, all the while allowing his worthy and admirable burden to sink lower and dispread in excess upon the surface of the water, until the vantage of her daughter's help was lost to her; I beheld the consequences of my indiscretion, dismayed. I would have checked the preposterous Virgilian, but in contempt of my uplifted hand and averted head, and regardless of the fact that his wife was then literally dependent upon him, the vicar declaimed (and the drenching effect produced by Latin upon a lady at such a season, may be thought on):

> Vix primos inopina quies laxaverat artus,
> Et super incumbens, cum puppis parte revulsa
> Cumque gubernaclo liquidas projecit in undas.'

It is not easy when you are unacquainted with the language, to retort upon Latin, even when the attempt to do so is made in English. Very few even of the uneducated ears can tolerate such anti-climax vituperative as English after sounding Latin. Mrs. Amble kept down those sentiments which her vernacular might have expressed. I heard but one groan that came from her as she lay huddled indistinguishably in the arms of her husband.

'Not—praecipitem! I am happy to say,' my senseless friend remarked further, and laughed cheerfully as he fortified his statement with a run of negatives. 'No, no'; in a way peculiar to him. 'No, no. If I plant my grey hairs anywhere, it will be on dry land: no. But, now, my dear; he returned to his duty; why, you're down again. Come: one, two, and up.'

He was raising a dead weight. The passion for sarcastic speech was manifestly at war with common prudence in the bosom of Mrs. Amble; prudence, however, overcame it. She cast on him a look of a kind that makes matrimony terrific in the dreams of bachelors, and then wedding her energy to the assistance given she made one of those senseless springs of the upper half of the body, which strike the philosophic eye with the futility of an effort that does not arise from a solid basis. Owing to the want of concert between them, the vicar's impulsive strength was expended when his wife's came into play. Alice clutched her mother bravely. The vicar had force enough to stay his wife's descent; but Alice (she boasts of her muscle) had not the force in the other direction—and no wonder. There are few young ladies who could pull fourteen stone sheer up a camshot.

Mrs. Amble remained in suspense between the two.

Oh, Mr. Pollingray, if you were only on this side to help us,' Miss Alice exclaimed very piteously, though I could see that she was half mad with the internal struggle of laughter at the parents and concern for them.

'Now, pull, Alice,' shouted the vicar.

'No, not yet,' screamed Mrs. Amble; I'm sinking.'

'Pull, Alice.'

'Now, Mama.'

'Oh!'

'Push, Papa.'

'I'm down.'

'Up, Ma'am; Jane; woman, up.'

'Gently, Papa: Abraham, I will not.'

'My dear, but you must.'

'And that man opposite.'

'What, Pollingray? He's fifty.'

I found myself walking indignantly down the path. Even now I protest my friend was guilty of bad manners, though I make every allowance for him; I excuse, I pass the order; but why—what justifies one man's bawling out another man's age? What purpose does it serve? I suppose the vicar wished to reassure his wife, on the principle (I have heard him enunciate it) that the sexes are merged at fifty—by which he means, I must presume, that something which may be good or bad, and is generally silly—of course, I admire and respect modesty and pudeur as much as any man—something has gone: a recognition of the bounds of division. There is, if that is a lamentable matter, a loss of certain of our young tricks at fifty. We have ceased to blush readily: and let me ask you to define a blush. Is it an involuntary truth or an ingenuous lie? I know that this will sound like the language of a man not a little jealous of his youthful compeers. I can but leave it to rightly judging persons to consider whether a healthy man in his prime, who has enough, and is not cursed by ambition, need be jealous of any living soul.

A shriek from Miss Alice checked my retreating steps. The vicar was staggering to support the breathing half of his partner while she regained her footing in the bed of the river. Their effort to scale the camshot had failed. Happily at this moment I caught sight of Master Frank's boat, which had floated, bottom upwards, against a projecting mud-bank of forget-me-nots. I contrived to reach it and right it, and having secured one of the sculls, I pulled up to the rescue; though not before I had plucked a flower, actuated by a motive that I cannot account for. The vicar held the boat firmly against the camshot, while I, at the imminent risk of joining them (I shall not forget the combined expression of Miss Alice's retreating eyes and the malicious corners of her mouth) hoisted the lady in, and the river with her. From the seat of the boat she stood sufficiently high to project the step towards land without peril. When she had set her foot there, we all assumed an attitude of respectful attention, and the vicar, who could soar over calamity like a fairweather swallow, acknowledged the return of his wife to the element with a series of apologetic yesses and short coughings.

'That would furnish a good concert for the poets,' he remarked. 'A parting, a separation of lovers; "even as a body from the watertorn," or "from the water plucked"; eh? do you think—"so I weep round her, tearful in her track," an excellent—'

But the outraged woman, dripping in grievous discomfort above him, made a peremptory gesture.

'Mr. Amble, will you come on shore instantly, I have borne with your stupidity long enough. I insist upon your remembering, sir, that you have a family dependent upon you. Other men may commit these follies.'

This was a blow at myself, a bachelor whom the lady had never persuaded to dream of relinquishing his freedom.

'My dear, I am coming,' said the vicar.

'Then, come at once, or I shall think you idiotic,' the wife retorted.

'I have been endeavouring,' the vicar now addressed me, 'to prove by a practical demonstration that women are capable of as much philosophy as men, under any sudden and afflicting revolution of circumstances.'

'And if you get a sunstroke, you will be rightly punished, and I shall not be sorry, Mr. Amble.'

'I am coming, my dear Jane. Pray run into the house and change your things.'

'Not till I see you out of the water, sir.'

'You are losing your temper, my love.'

'You would make a saint lose his temper, Mr. Amble.'

'There were female saints, my dear,' the vicar mildly responded; and addressed me further: 'Up to this point, I assure you, Pollingray, no conduct could have been more exemplary than Mrs. Amble's. I had got her into the boat—a good boat, a capital boat—but getting in myself, we overturned. The first impulse of an ordinary woman would have been to reproach and scold; but Mrs. Amble succumbed only to the first impulse. Discovering that all effort unaided to climb the bank was fruitless, she agreed to wait patiently and make the best of circumstances; and she did; and she learnt to enjoy it. There is marrow in every bone. My dear. Jane, I have never admired you so much. I tried her, Pollingray, in metaphysics. I talked to her of the opera we last heard, I think fifty years ago. And as it is less endurable for a woman to be patient in tribulation—the honour is greater, when she overcomes the fleshy trial. Insomuch,' the vicar put on a bland air of abnegation of honour, 'that I am disposed to consider any male philosopher our superior; when you've found one, ha, ha—when you've found one. O sol pulcher! I am ready to sing that the day has been glorious, so far. Pulcher ille dies.'

Mrs. Amble appealed to me. 'Would anybody not swear that he is mad to see him standing waist-deep in the water and the sun on his bald head, I am reduced to entreat you not to—though you have no family of your own—not to encourage him. It is amusing to you. Pray, reflect that such folly is too often fatal. Compel him to come on shore.'

The logic of the appeal was no doubt distinctly visible in the lady's mind, though it was not accurately worded. I saw that I stood marked to be the scape goat of the day, and humbly continued to deserve well, notwithstanding. By dint of simple signs and nods of affirmative, and a constant propulsion of my friend's arm, I drew him into the boat, and thence projected him up to the level with his wife, who had perhaps deigned to understand that it was best to avoid the arresting of his divergent mind by any remark during the passage, and remained silent. No sooner was he established on his feet, than she plucked him away.

'Your papa's hat,' she called, flashing to her daughter, and streamed up the lawn into the rose-trellised pathways leading on aloft to the vicarage house. Behind roses the weeping couple disappeared. The last I saw of my friend was a smiting of his hand upon his head in a vain effort to catch at one of the fleeting ideas sowed in him by the quick passage of objects before his vision, and shaken out of him by abnormal hurry. The Rev. Abraham Amble had been lord of his wife in the water, but his innings was over. He had evidently enjoyed it vastly, and I now understood why he had chosen to prolong it as much as possible. Your eccentric characters are not uncommonly amateurs of petty artifice. There are hours of vengeance even for henpecked men.

I found myself sighing over the enslaved condition of every Benedict of my acquaintance, when the thought came like a surprise that I was alone with Alice. The fair and pleasant damsel made a clever descent into the boat, and having seated herself, she began to twirl the scull in the rowlock, and said: 'Do you feel disposed to join me in looking after the other scull and papa's hat, Mr. Pollingray?' I suggested 'Will you not get your feet wet? I couldn't manage to empty all the water in the boat.'

'Oh' cried she, with a toss of her head; I wet feet never hurt young people.'

There was matter for an admonitory lecture in this. Let me confess I was about to give it, when she added: But Mr. Pollingray, I am really afraid that your feet are wet! You had to step into the water when you righted the boat:

My reply was to jump down by her side with as much agility as I could combine with a proper discretion. The amateur craft rocked threateningly, and I found myself grasped by and grasping the pretty damsel, until by great good luck we were steadied and preserved from the same misfortune which had befallen her parents. She laughed and blushed, and we tottered asunder.

'Would you have talked metaphysics to me in the water, Mr. Pollingray?'

Alice was here guilty of one of those naughty sort of innocent speeches smacking of Eve most strongly; though, of course, of Eve in her best days.

I took the rudder lines to steer against the sculling of her single scull, and was Adam enough to respond to temptation: 'I should perhaps have been grateful to your charitable construction of it as being metaphysics.'

She laughed colloquially, to fill a pause. It had not been coquetry: merely the woman unconsciously at play. A man is bound to remember the seniority of his years when this occurs, for a veteran of ninety and a worn out young debauchee will equally be subject to it if they do not shun the society of the sex. My long robust health and perfect self-reliance apparently tend to give me unguarded moments, or lay me open to fitful impressions. Indeed there are times when I fear I have the heart of a boy, and certainly nothing more calamitous can be conceived, supposing that it should ever for one instant get complete mastery of my head. This is the peril of a man who has lived soberly. Do we never know when we are safe? I am, in reflecting thereupon, positively prepared to say that if there is no fool like what they call an old fool (and a man in his prime, who can be laughed at, is the world's old fool) there is wisdom in the wild oats theory, and I shall come round to my nephew's way of thinking: that is, as far as Master Charles by his acting represents his thinking. I shall at all events be more lenient in my judgement of him, and less stern in my allocutions, for I shall have no text to preach from.

We picked up the hat and the scull in one of the little muddy bays of our brown river, forming an amphitheatre for water-rats and draped with great dockleaves, nettle-flowers, ragged robins, and other weeds for which the learned young lady gave the botanical names. It was pleasant to hear her speak with the full authority of absolute knowledge of her subject. She has intelligence. She is decidedly too good for Charles, unless he changes his method of living.

'Shall we row on?' she asked, settling her arms to work the pair of sculls.

'You have me in your power,' said I, and she struck out. Her shape is exceedingly graceful; I was charmed by the occasional tightening in of her lips as she exerted her muscle, while at intervals telling me of her race with one of her boastful younger brothers, whom she had beaten. I believe it is only when they are using physical exertion that the eyes of young girls have entire simplicity—the simplicity of nature as opposed to that other artificial simplicity which they learn from their governesses, their mothers, and the admiration of witlings. Attractive purity, or the nice glaze of no comprehension of anything which is considered to be improper in a wicked world, and is no doubt very useful, is not to my taste. French girls, as a rule, cannot compete with our English in the purer graces. They are only incomparable when as women they have resort to art.

Alice could look at me as she rowed, without thinking it necessary to force a smile, or to speak, or to snigger and be foolish. I felt towards the girl like a comrade.

We went no further than Hatchard's mile, where the water plumps the poor sleepy river from a sidestream, and, as it turned the boat's head quite round, I lct the boat go. These studies of young women are very well as a pastime; but they soon cease to be a recreation. She forms an agreeable picture when she is rowing, and possesses a musical laugh. Now and then she gives way to the bad trick of laughing without caring or daring to explain the cause for it. She is moderately well-bred. I hope that she has principle. Certain things a man of my time of life learns by associating with very young people which are serviceable to him. What a different matter this earth must be to that girl from what it is to me! I knew it before. And—mark the difference—I feel it now.

Chapter 2

She

Papa never will cease to meet with accidents and adventures. If he only walks out to sit for half an hour with one of his old dames, as he calls them, something is sure to happen to him, and it is almost as sure that Mr. Pollingray will be passing at the time and mixed up in it.

Since Mr. Pollingray's return from his last residence on the Continent, I have learnt to know him and like him. Charles is unjust to his uncle. He is not at all the grave kind of man I expected from Charles's description. He is extremely entertaining, and then he understands the world, and I like to hear him talk, he is so unpretentious and uses just the right words. No one would imagine his age, from his appearance, and he has more fun than any young man I have listened to.

But, I am convinced I have discovered his weakness. It is my fatal peculiarity that I cannot be with people ten minutes without seeing some point about them where they are tenderest. Mr. Pollingray wants to be thought quite youthful. He can bear any amount of fatigue; he is always fresh and a delightful companion; but you cannot get him to show even a shadow of exhaustion or to admit that he ever knew what it was to lie down beaten. This is really to pretend that he is superhuman. I like him so much that I could wish him superior to such—it is nothing other than—vanity. Which is worse? A young man giving himself the air of a sage, or—but no one can call Mr. Pollingray an old man. He is a confirmed bachelor. That puts the case. Charles, when he says of him that he is a 'gentleman in a good state of preservation,' means to be ironical. I doubt whether Charles at fifty would object to have the same said of Mr. Charles Everett. Mr. Pollingray has always looked to his health. He has not been disappointed. I am sure he was always very good. But, whatever he was, he is now very pleasant, and he does not talk to women as if he thought them singular, and feel timid, I mean, confused, as some men show that they feel—the good ones. Perhaps he felt so once, and that is why he is still free. Charles's dread that his uncle will marry is most unworthy. He never will, but why should he not? Mama declares that he is waiting for a woman of intellect, I can hear her: 'Depend upon it, a woman of intellect will marry Dayton Manor.' Should that mighty event not come to pass, poor Charles will have to sink the name of Everett in that of Pollingray. Mr. Pollingray's name is the worst thing about him. When I think of his name I see him ten times older than he is. My feelings are in harmony with his pedigree concerning the age of the name. One would have to be a woman of profound intellect to see the advantage of sharing it.

'Mrs. Pollingray!' She must be a lady with a wig.

It was when we were rowing up by Hatchard's mill that I first perceived his weakness, he was looking at me so kindly, and speaking of his friendship for papa, and how glad he was to be fixed at last, near to us at Dayton. I wished to use some term of endearment in reply, and said, I remember, 'Yes, and we are also glad, Godpapa.' I was astonished that he should look so disconcerted, and went on: 'Have you forgotten that you are my godpapa?'

He answered: 'Am I? Oh! yes—the name of Alice.'

Still he looked uncertain, uncomfortable, and I said, 'Do you want to cancel the past, and cast me off?'

'No, certainly not'; he, I suppose, thought he was assuring me.

I saw his lips move at the words I cancel the past,' though he did not speak them out. He positively blushed. I know the sort of young man he must have been. Exactly the sort of young man mama would like for a son-in-law, and her daughters would accept in pure obedience when reduced to be capable of the virtue by rigorous diet, or consumption.

He let the boat go round instantly. This was enough for me. It struck me then that when papa had said to mama (as he did in that absurd situation) 'He is fifty,' Mr. Pollingray must have heard it across the river, for he walked away hurriedly. He came back, it is true, with the boat, but I have my own ideas. He is always ready to do a service, but on this occasion I think it was an afterthought. I shall not venture to call him 'Godpapa' again.

Indeed, if I have a desire, it is that I may be blind to people's weakness. My insight is inveterate. Papa says he has heard Mr. Pollingray boast of his age. If so, there has come a change over him. I cannot be deceived. I see it constantly. After my unfortunate speech, Mr. Pollingray shunned our house for two whole weeks, and scarcely bowed to us when coming out of church. Miss Pollingray idolises him—spoils him. She says that he is worth twenty of Charles. Nous savons ce que nous savons, nous autres. Charles is wild, but Charles would be above these littlenesses. How could Miss Pollingray comprehend the romance of Charles's nature?

My sister Evelina is now Mr. Pollingray's favourite. She could not say Godpapa to him, if she would. Persons who are very much petted at home, are always establishing favourites abroad. For my part, let them praise me or not, I know that I can do any thing I set my mind upon. At present I choose to be frivolous. I know I am frivolous. What then? If there is fun in the world am I not to laugh at it? I shall astonish them by and by. But, I will laugh while I can. I am sure, there is so much misery in the world, it is a mercy to be able to laugh. Mr. Pollingray may think what he likes of me. When Charles tells me that I must do my utmost to propitiate his uncle, he cannot mean that I am to refrain from laughing, because that is being a hypocrite, which I may become when I have gone through all the potential moods and not before.

It is preposterous to suppose that I am to be tied down to the views of life of elderly people.

I dare say I did laugh a little too much the other night, but could I help it? We had a dinner party. Present were Mr. Pollingray, Mrs. Kershaw, the Wilbury people (three), Charles, my brother Duncan, Evelina, mama, papa, myself, and Mr. and Mrs. (put them last for emphasis) Romer Pattlecombe, Mrs. Pattlecombe (the same number of syllables as Pollingray, and a 'P' to begin with) is thirty-one years her husband's junior, and she is twenty-six; full of fun, and always making fun of him, the mildest, kindest, goody old thing, who has never distressed himself for anything and never will. Mrs. Romer not only makes fun, but is fun. When you have done laughing with her, you can laugh at her. She is the salt of society in these parts. Some one, as we were sitting on the lawn after dinner, alluded to the mishap to papa and mama, and mama, who has never forgiven Mr. Pollingray for having seen her in her ridiculous plight, said that men were in her opinion greater gossips than women. 'That is indisputable, ma'am,' said Mr. Pollingray, he loves to bewilder her; 'only, we never mention it.'

'There is an excuse for us,' said Mrs. Romer; 'our trials are so great, we require a diversion, and so we talk of others.'

'Now really,' said Charles, 'I don't think your trials are equal to ours.'

For which remark papa bantered him, and his uncle was sharp on him; and Charles, I know, spoke half seriously, though he was seeking to draw Mrs. Romer out: he has troubles.

From this, we fell upon a comparison of sufferings, and Mrs. Romer took up the word. She is a fair, smallish, nervous woman, with delicate hands and outlines, exceedingly sympathetic; so much so that while you are telling her anything, she makes half a face in anticipation, and is ready to shriek with laughter or shake her head with uttermost grief; and sometimes, if you let her go too far in one direction, she does both. All her narrations are with ups and downs of her hands, her eyes, her chin, and her voice. Taking poor, good old Mr. Romer by the roll of his coat, she made as if posing him, and said: 'There! Now, it's all very well for you to say that there is anything equal to a woman's sufferings in this world. I do declare you know nothing of what we unhappy women have to endure. It's dreadful! No male creature can possibly know what tortures I have to undergo.'

Mama neatly contrived, after interrupting her, to divert the subject. I think that all the ladies imagined they were in jeopardy, but I knew Mrs. Romer was perfectly to be trusted. She has wit which pleases, jusqu'aux ongles, and her sense of humour never overrides her discretion with more than a glance—never with preparation.

'Now,' she pursued, 'let me tell you what excruciating trials I have to go through. This man,' she rocked the patient old gentleman to and fro, 'this man will be the death of me. He is utterly devoid of a sense of propriety. Again and again I say to him—cannot the tailor cut down these trowsers of yours? Yes, Mr. Amble, you preach patience to women, but this is too much for any woman's endurance. Now, do attempt to picture to yourself what an agony it must be to me:—he will shave, and he will wear those enormously high trowsers that, when they are braced, reach up behind to the nape of his neck! Only yesterday morning, as I was lying in bed, I could see him in his dressing-room. I tell you: he will shave, and he will choose the time for shaving early after he has braced these immensely high trowsers that make such a placard of him. Oh, my goodness! My dear Romer, I have said to him fifty times if I have said it once, my goodness me! why can you not get decent trowsers such as other men wear? He has but one answer—he has been accustomed to wear those trowsers, and he would not feel at home in another pair. And what does he say if I continue to complain? and I cannot but continue to complain, for it is not only moral, it is physical torment to see the sight he makes of himself; he says: "My dear, you should not have married an old man." What! I say to him, must an old man wear antiquated trowsers? No! nothing will turn him; those are his habits. But, you have not heard the worst. The sight of those hideous trowsers totally destroying all shape in the man, is horrible enough; but it is absolutely more than a woman can bear to see him—for he will shave—first cover his face with white soap with that ridiculous centre-piece to his trowsers reaching quite up to his poll, and then, you can fancy a woman's rage and anguish! the figure lifts its nose by the extremist tip. Oh! it's degradation! What respect can a woman have for her husband after that sight? Imagine it! And I have implored him to spare me. It's useless. You sneer at our hbops and say that you are inconvenienced by them but you gentlemen are not degraded,—Oh! unutterably!—as I am every morning of my life by that cruel spectacle of a husband.'

I have but faintly sketched Mrs. Romer's style. Evelina, who is prudish and thinks her vulgar, refused to laugh, but it came upon me, as the picture of 'your own old husband,' with so irresistibly comic an effect that I was overcome by convulsions of laughter. I do not defend myself. It was as much a fit as any other attack. I did all I could to arrest it. At last, I ran indoors and upstairs to my bedroom and tried hard to become dispossessed. I am sure I was an example of the sufferings of my sex. It could hardly have been worse for Mrs. Romer than it was for me. I was drowned in internal laughter long after I had got a grave face. Early in the evening Mr. Pollingray left us.

Chapter 3

He

I am carried by the fascination of a musical laugh. Apparently I am doomed to hear it at my own expense. We are secure from nothing in this life.

I have determined to stand for the county. An unoccupied man is a prey to every hook of folly. Be dilettante all your days, and you might as fairly hope to reap a moral harvest as if you had chased butterflies. The activities created by a profession or determined pursuit are necessary to the growth of the mind.

Heavens! I find myself writing like an illegitimate son of La Rochefoucauld, or of Vauvenargues. But, it is true that I am fifty years old, and I am not mature. I am undeveloped somewhere.

The question for me to consider is, whether this development is to be accomplished by my being guilty of an act of egregious folly.

Dans la cinquantaine! The reflection should produce a gravity in men. Such a number of years will not ring like bridal bells in a man's ears. I have my books about me, my horses, my dogs, a contented household. I move in the centre of a perfect machine, and I am dissatisfied. I rise early. I do not digest badly. What is wrong?

The calamity of my case is that I am in danger of betraying what is wrong with me to others, without knowing it myself. Some woman will be suspecting and tattling, because she has nothing else to do. Girls have wonderfully shrewd eyes for a weakness in the sex which they are instructed to look upon as superior. But I am on my guard.

The fact is manifest: I feel I have been living more or less uselessly. It is a fat time. There are a certain set of men in every prosperous country who, having wherewithal, and not being compelled to toil, become subjected to the moral ideal. Most of them in the end sit down with our sixth Henry or second Richard and philosophise on shepherds. To be no better than a simple hind! Am I better? Prime bacon and an occasional draft of shrewd beer content him, and they do not me. Yet I am sound, and can sit through the night and be ready, and on the morrow I shall stand for the county.

I made the announcement that I had thoughts of entering Parliament, before I had half formed the determination, at my sister's lawn party yesterday.

'Gilbert!' she cried, and raised her hands. A woman is hurt if you do not confide to her your plans as soon as you can conceive them. She must be present to assist at the birth, or your plans are unblessed plans.

I had been speaking aside in a casual manner to my friend Amble, whose idea is that the Church is not represented with sufficient strength in the Commons, and who at once, as I perceived, grasped the notion of getting me to promote sundry measures connected with schools and clerical stipends, for his eyes dilated; he said: 'Well, if you do, I can put you up to several things,' and imparting the usual chorus of yesses to his own mind, he continued absently: 'Pollingray might be made strong on church rates. There is much to do. He has lived abroad and requires schooling in these things. We want a man. Yes, yes, yes. It's a good idea; a notion.'

My sister, however, was of another opinion. She did me the honour to take me aside.

'Gilbert, were you serious just now?'

'Quite serious. Is it not my characteristic?'

'Not on these occasions. I saw the idea come suddenly upon you. You were looking at Charles.'

'Continue: and at what was he looking?'

'He was looking at Alice Amble.'

'And the young lady?'

'She looked at you.'

I was here attacked by a singularly pertinacious fly, and came out of the contest with a laugh.

'Did she have that condescension towards me? And from the glance, my resolution to enter Parliament was born? It is the French vaudevilliste's doctrine of great events from little causes. The slipper of a soubrette trips the heart of a king and changes the destiny of a nation-the history of mankind. It may be true. If I were but shot into the House from a little girl's eye!'

With this I took her arm gaily, walked with her, and had nearly overreached myself with excess of cunning. I suppose we are reduced to see more plainly that which we systematically endeavour to veil from others. It is best to flutter a handkerchief, instead of nailing up a curtain. The principal advantage is that you may thereby go on deceiving yourself, for this reason: few sentiments are wholly matter of fact; but when they are half so, you make them concrete by deliberately seeking either to crush or conceal them, and you are doubly betrayed—betrayed to the besieging eye and to yourself. When a sentiment has grown to be a passion (mercifully may I be spared!) different tactics are required. By that time, you will have already betrayed yourself too deeply to dare to be flippant: the investigating eye is aware that it has been purposely diverted: knowing some things, it makes sure of the rest from which you turn it away. If you want to hide a very grave case, you must speak gravely about it.—At which season, be but sure of your voice, and simulate a certain depth of sentimental philosophy, and you may once more, and for a long period, bewilder the investigator of the secrets of your bosom. To sum up: in the preliminary stages of a weakness, be careful that you do not show your own alarm, or all will be suspected. Should the weakness turn to fever, let a little of it be seen, like a careless man, and nothing will really be thought.

I can say this, I can do this; and is it still possible that a pin's point has got through the joints of the armour of a man like me?

Elizabeth quitted my side with the conviction that I am as considerate an uncle as I am an affectionate brother.

I said to her, apropos, 'I have been observing those two. It seems to me they are deciding things for themselves.'

'I have been going to speak to you about them Gilbert,' said she.

And I: 'The girl must be studied. The family is good. While Charles is in Wales, you must have her at Dayton. She laughs rather vacantly, don't you think? but the sound of it has the proper wholesome ring. I will give her what attention I can while she is here, but in the meantime I must have a bride of my own and commence courting.'

'Parliament, you mean,' said Elizabeth with a frank and tender smile. The hostess was summoned to welcome a new guest, and she left me, pleased with her successful effort to reach my meaning, and absorbed by it.

I would not have challenged Machiavelli; but I should not have encountered the Florentine ruefully. I feel the same keen delight in intellectual dexterity. On some points my sister is not a bad match for me. She can beat me seven games out of twelve at chess; but the five I win sequently, for then I am awake. There is natural art and artificial art, and the last beats the first. Fortunately for us, women are strangers to the last. They have had to throw off a mask before they have, got the schooling; so, when they are thus armed we know what we meet, and what are the weapons to be used.

Alice, if she is a fine fencer at all, will expect to meet the ordinary English squire in me. I have seen her at the baptismal font! It is inconceivable. She will fancy that at least she is ten times more subtle than I. When I get the mastery—it is unlikely to make me the master. What may happen is, that the nature of the girl will declare itself, under the hard light of intimacy, vulgar. Charles I cause to be absent for six weeks; so there will be time enough for the probation. I do not see him till he returns. If by chance I had come earlier to see him and he to allude to her, he would have had my conscience on his side, and that is what a scrupulous man takes care to prevent.

I wonder whether my friends imagine me to be the same man whom they knew as Gilbert Pollingray a month back? I see the change, I feel the change; but I have no retrospection, no remorse, no looking forward, no feeling: none for others, very little, for myself. I am told that I am losing fluency as a dinner-table talker. There is now more savour to me in a silvery laugh than in a spiced wit. And this is the man who knows women, and is far too modest to give a decided opinion upon any of their merits. Search myself through as I may, I cannot tell when the change began, or what the change consists of, or what is the matter with me, or what charm there is in the person who does the mischief. She is the counterpart of dozens of girls; lively, brown-eyed, brown-haired, underbred—it is not too harsh to say so—underbred slightly; half-educated, whether quickwitted I dare not opine. She is undoubtedly the last whom I or another person would have fixed upon as one to work me this unmitigated evil. I do not know her, and I believe I do not care to know her, and I am thirsting for the hour to come when I shall study her. Is not this to have the poison of a bite in one's blood? The wrath of Venus is not a fable. I was a hard reader and I despised the sex in my youth, before the family estates fell to me; since when I have playfully admired the sex; I have dallied with a passion, and not read at all, save for diversion: her anger is not a fable. You may interpret many a mythic tale by the facts which lie in your own blood. My emotions have lain altogether dormant in sentimental attachment. I have, I suppose, boasted of, Python slain, and Cupid has touched me up with an arrow. I trust to my own skill rather than to his mercy for avoiding a second from his quiver. I will understand this girl if I have to submit to a close intimacy with her for six months. There is no doubt of the elegance of her movements. Charles might as well take his tour, and let us see him again next year. Yes, her movements are (or will be) gracious. In a year's time she will have acquired the fuller tones and poetry of womanliness. Perhaps then, too, her smile will linger instead of flashing. I have known infinitely lovelier women than she. One I have known! but let her be. Louise and I have long since said adieu.

Chapter 4

She

Behold me installed in Dayton Manor House, and brought here for the express purpose (so Charles has written me word) of my being studied, that it may be seen whether I am worthy to be, on some august future occasion—possibly—a member (Oh, so much to mumble!) of this great family. Had I known it when I was leaving home, I should have countermanded the cording of my boxes. If you please, I do the packing, and not the cording. I must practise being polite, or I shall be horrifying these good people.

I am mortally offended. I am very very angry. I shall show temper. Indeed, I have shown it. Mr. Pollingray must and does think me a goose. Dear sir, and I think you are justified. If any one pretends to guess how, I have names to suit that person. I am a ninny, an ape, and mind I call myself these bad things because I deserve worse. I am flighty, I believe I am heartless. Charles is away, and I suffer no pangs. The truth is, I fancied myself so exceedingly penetrating, and it was my vanity looking in a glass. I saw something that answered to my nods and howd'ye-do's and—but I am ashamed, and so penitent I might begin making a collection of beetles. I cannot lift up my head.

Mr. Pollingray is such a different man from the one I had imagined! What that one was, I have now quite forgotten. I remember too clearly what the wretched guesser was. I have been three weeks at Dayton, and if my sisters know me when I return to the vicarage, they are not foolish virgins. For my part, I know that I shall always hate Mrs. Romer Pattlecombe, and that I am unjust to the good woman, but I do hate her, and I think the stories shocking, and wonder intensely what it was that I could have found in them to laugh at. I shall never laugh again for many years. Perhaps, when I am an old woman, I may. I wish the time had come. All young people seem to me so helplessly silly. I am one of them for the present, and have no hope that I can appear to be anything else. The young are a crowd—a shoal of small fry. Their elders are the select of the world.

On the morning of the day when I was to leave home for Dayton, a distance of eight miles, I looked out of my window while dressing—as early as halfpast seven—and I saw Mr. Pollingray's groom on horseback, leading up and down the walk a darling little, round, plump, black cob that made my heart leap with an immense bound of longing to be on it and away across the downs. And then the maid came to my door with a letter:

'Mr. Pollingray, in return for her considerate good behaviour and saving of trouble to him officially, begs his goddaughter to accept the accompanying little animal: height 14 h., age 31 years; hunts, is sure-footed, and likely to be the best jumper in the county.'

I flew downstairs. I rushed out of the house and up to my treasure, and kissed his nose and stroked his mane. I could not get my fingers away from him. Horses are so like the very best and beautifullest of women when you caress them. They show their pleasure so at being petted. They curve their necks, and paw, and look proud. They take your flattery like sunshine and are lovely in it. I kissed my beauty, peering at his black-mottled skin, which is like Allingborough Heath in the twilight. The smell of his new saddle and bridle-leather was sweeter than a garden to me. The man handed me a large riding-whip mounted with silver. I longed to jump up and ride till midnight.

Then mama and papa came out and read the note and looked, at my darling little cob, and my sisters saw him and kissed me, for they are not envious girls. The most distressing thing was that we had not a riding-habit in the family. I was ready to wear any sort. I would have ridden as a guy rather than not ride at all. But mama gave me a promise that in two days a riding-habit should be sent on to Dayton, and I had to let my pet be led back from where he came. I had no life till I was following him. I could have believed him to be a fairy prince who had charmed me. I called him Prince Leboo, because he was black and good. I forgive anybody who talks about first love after what my experience has been with Prince Leboo.

What papa thought of the present I do not know, but I know very well what mama thought: and for my part I thought everything, not distinctly including that, for I could not suppose such selfishness in one so generous as Mr. Pollingray. But I came to Dayton in a state of arrogant pride, that gave assurance if not ease to my manners. I thanked Mr. Pollingray warmly, but in a way to let him see it was the matter of a horse between us. 'You give, I register thanks, and there's an end.'

'He thinks me a fool! a fool!'

'My habit,' I said, 'comes after me. I hope we shall have some rides together.'

'Many,' replied Mr. Pollingray, and his bow inflated me with ideas of my condescension.

And because Miss Pollingray (Queen Elizabeth he calls her) looked half sad, I read it—! I do not write what I read it to be.

Behold the uttermost fool of all female creation led over the house by Mr. Pollingray. He showed me the family pictures.

'I am no judge of pictures, Mr. Pollingray.'

'You will learn to see the merits of these.'

'I'm afraid not, though I were to study them for years.'

'You may have that opportunity.'

'Oh! that is more than I can expect.'

'You will develop intelligence on such subjects by and by.'

A dull sort of distant blow struck me in this remark; but I paid no heed to it.

He led me over the gardens and the grounds. The Great John Methlyn Pollingray planted those trees, and designed the house, and the flower-garden still speaks of his task; but he is not my master, and consequently I could not share his three great-grandsons' veneration for him. There are high fir-woods and beech woods, and a long ascending narrow meadow between them, through which a brook falls in continual cascades. It is the sort of scene I love, for it has a woodland grandeur and seclusion that leads, me to think, and makes a better girl of me. But what I said was: 'Yes, it is the place of all others to come and settle in for the evening of one's days.'

'You could not take to it now?' said Mr. Pollingray.

'Now?' my expression of face must have been a picture.

'You feel called upon to decline such a residence in the morning of your days?'

He persisted in looking at me as he spoke, and I felt like something withering scarlet.

I am convinced he saw through me, while his face was polished brass. My self-possession returned, for my pride was not to be dispersed immediately.

'Please, take me to the stables,' I entreated; and there I was at home. There I saw my Prince Leboo, and gave him a thousand caresses.'

'He knows me already,' I said.

Then he is some degrees in advance of me,' said Mr. Pollingray.

Is not cold dissection of one's character a cruel proceeding? And I think, too, that a form of hospitality like this by which I am invited to be analysed at leisure, is both mean and base. I have been kindly treated and I am grateful, but I do still say (even though I may have improved under it) it is unfair.

To proceed: the dinner hour arrived. The atmosphere of his own house seems to favour Mr. Pollingray as certain soils and sites favour others. He walked into the dining-room between us with his hands behind him, talking to us both so easily and smoothly cheerfully—naturally and pleasantly—inimitable by any young man! You hardly feel the change of room. We were but three at table, but there was no lack of entertainment. Mr. Pollingray is an admirable host; he talks just enough himself and helps you to talk. What does comfort me is that it gives him real pleasure to see a hearty appetite. Young men, I know it for a certainty, never quite like us to be so human. Ah! which is right? I would not miss the faith in our nobler essence which Charles has. But, if it nobler? One who has lived longer in the world ought to know better, and Mr. Pollingray approves of naturalness in everything. I have now seen through Charles's eyes for several months; so implicitly that I am timid when I dream of trusting to another's judgement. It is, however, a fact that I am not quite natural with Charles.

Every day Mr. Pollingray puts on evening dress out of deference to his sister. If young men had these good habits they would gain our respect, and lose their own self-esteem less early.

After dinner I sang. Then Mr. Pollingray read an amusing essay to us, and retired to his library. Miss Pollingray sat and talked to me of her brother, and of her nephew—for whom it is that Mr. Pollingray is beginning to receive company, and is going into society. Charles's subsequently received letter explained the 'receive company.' I could not comprehend it at the time.

'The house has been shut up for years, or rarely inhabited by us for more than a month in the year. Mr. Pollingray prefers France. All his associations, I may say his sympathies, are in France. Latterly he seems to have changed a little; but from Normandy to Touraine and Dauphiny—we had a triangular home over there. Indeed, we have it still. I am never certain of my brother.'

While Miss Pollingray was speaking, my eyes were fixed on a Vidal crayon drawing, faintly coloured with chalks, of a foreign lady—I could have sworn to her being French—young, quite girlish, I doubt if her age was more than mine.

She is pretty, is she not?' said Miss Pollingray.

She is almost beautiful,' I exclaimed, and Miss Pollingray, seeing my curiosity, was kind enough not to keep me in suspense.

'That is the Marquise de Mazardouin—nee Louise de Riverolles. You will see other portraits of her in the house. This is the most youthful of them, if I except one representing a baby, and bearing her initials.'

I remembered having noticed a similarity of feature in some of the portraits in the different rooms. My longing to look at them again was like a sudden jet of flame within me. There was no chance of seeing them till morning; so, promising myself to dream of the face before me, I dozed through a conversation with my hostess, until I had got the French lady's eyes and hair and general outline stamped accurately, as I hoped, on my mind. I was no sooner on my way to bed than all had faded. The torment of trying to conjure up that face was inconceivable. I lay, and tossed, and turned to right and to left, and scattered my sleep; but by and by my thoughts reverted to Mr. Pollingray, and then like sympathetic ink held to the heat, I beheld her again; but vividly, as she must have been when she was sitting to the artist. The hair was naturally crisped, waving thrice over the forehead and brushed clean from the temples, showing the small ears, and tied in a knot loosely behind. Her eyebrows were thick and dark, but soft; flowing eyebrows; far lovelier, to my thinking, than any pencilled arch. Dark eyes, and full, not prominent. I find little expression of inward sentiment in very prominent eyes. On the contrary they seem to have a fish-like dependency of gaze on what is without, and show fishy depths, if any. For instance, my eyes are rather prominent, and I am just the little fool—but the French lady is my theme. Madame la Marquise, your eyes are sweeter to me than celestial. I never saw such candour and unaffected innocence in eyes before. Accept the compliment of the pauvre Anglaise. Did you do mischief with them? Did Vidal's delicate sketch do justice to you? Your lips and chin and your throat all repose in such girlish grace, that if ever it is my good fortune to see you, you will not be aged to me!

I slept and dreamed of her.

In the morning, I felt certain that she had often said: 'Mon cher Gilbert,' to Mr. Pollingray. Had he ever said: 'Ma chere Louise?' He might have said: 'Ma bien aimee!' for it was a face to be loved.

My change of feeling towards him dates from that morning. He had previously seemed to me a man so much older. I perceived in him now a youthfulness beyond mere vigour of frame. I could not detach him from my dreams of the night. He insists upon addressing me by the terms of our 'official' relationship, as if he made it a principle of our intercourse.

'Well, and is your godpapa to congratulate you on your having had a quiet rest?' was his greeting.

I answered stupidly: 'Oh, yes, thank you,' and would have given worlds for the courage to reply in French, but I distrusted my accent. At breakfast, the opportunity or rather the excuse for an attempt, was offered. His French valet, Francois, waits on him at breakfast. Mr. Pollingray and his sister asked for things in the French tongue, and, as if fearing some breach of civility, Mr. Pollingray asked me if I knew French.

Yes, I know it; that is, I understand it,' I stuttered. Allons, nous parlerons francais,' said he. But I shook my head, and remained like a silly mute.

I was induced towards the close of the meal to come out with a few French words. I was utterly shamefaced. Mr. Pollingray has got the French manner of protesting that one is all but perfect in one's speaking. I know how absurd it must have sounded. But I felt his kindness, and in my heart I thanked him humbly. I believe now that a residence in France does not deteriorate an Englishman. Mr. Pollingray, when in his own house, has the best qualities of the two countries. He is gay, and, yes, while he makes a study of me, I am making a study of him. Which of us two will know the other first? He was papa's college friend—papa's junior, of course, and infinitely more papa's junior now. I observe that weakness in him, I mean, his clinging to youthfulness, less and less; but I do see it, I cannot be quite in error. The truth is, I begin to feel that I cannot venture to mistrust my infallible judgement, or I shall have no confidence in myself at all.

After breakfast, I was handed over to Miss Pollingray, with the intimation that I should not see him till dinner.

'Gilbert is anxious to cultivate the society of his English neighbours, now that he has, as he supposes, really settled among them,' she remarked to me. 'At his time of life, the desire to be useful is almost a malady. But, he cherishes the poor, and that is more than an occupation, it is a virtue.'

Her speech has become occasionally French in the construction of the sentences.

'Mais oui,' I said shyly, and being alone with her, I was not rebuffed by her smile, especially as she encouraged me on.

I am, she told me, to see a monde of French people here in September. So, the story of me is to be completer, or continued in September. I could not get Miss Pollingray to tell me distinctly whether Madame la Marquise will be one of the guests. But I know that she is not a widow. In that case, she has a husband. In that case, what is the story of her relations towards Mr. Pollingray? There must be some story. He would not surely have so many portraits of her about the house (and they travel with him wherever he goes) if she were but a lovely face to him. I cannot understand it. They were frequent, constant visitors to one another's estates in France; always together. Perhaps a man of Mr. Pollingray's age, or perhaps M. le Marquis—and here I lose myself. French habits are so different from ours. One thing I am certain of: no charge can be brought against my Englishman. I read perfect rectitude in his face. I would cast anchor by him. He must have had a dreadful unhappiness.

Mama kept her promise by sending my riding habit and hat punctually, but I had run far ahead of all the wishes I had formed when I left home, and I half feared my ride out with Mr. Pollingray. That was before I had received Charles's letter, letting me know the object of my invitation here. I require at times a morbid pride to keep me up to the work. I suppose I rode befittingly, for Mr. Pollingray praised my seat on horseback. I know I can ride, or feel the 'blast of a horse like my own'—as he calls it. Yet he never could have had a duller companion. My conversation was all yes and no, as if it went on a pair of crutches like a miserable cripple. I was humiliated and vexed. All the while I was trying to lead up to the French lady, and I could not commence with a single question. He appears to, have really cancelled the past in every respect save his calling me his goddaughter. His talk was of the English poor, and vegetation, and papa's goodness to his old dames in Ickleworth parish, and defects in my education acknowledged by me, but not likely to restore me in my depressed state. The ride was beautiful. We went the length of a twelve-mile ridge between Ickleworth and Hillford, over high commons, with immense views on both sides, and through beech-woods, oakwoods, and furzy dells and downs spotted with juniper and yewtrees—old picnic haunts of mine, but Mr. Pollingray's fresh delight in the landscape made them seem new and strange. Home through the valley.

The next day Miss Pollingray joined us, wearing a feutre gris and green plume, which looked exceedingly odd until you became accustomed to it. Her hair has decided gray streaks, and that, and the Queen Elizabeth nose, and the feutre gris!—but she is so kind, I could not even smile in my heart. It is singular that Mr. Pollingray, who's but three years her junior, should look at least twenty years younger—at the very least. His moustache and beard are of the colour of a corn sheaf, and his blue eyes shining over them remind me of summer. That describes him. He is summer, and has not fallen into his autumn yet. Miss Pollingray helped me to talk a little. She tried to check her brother's enthusiasm for our scenery, and extolled the French paysage.

He laughed at her, for when they were in France it was she who used to say, 'There is nothing here like England!' Miss Fool rode between them attentive to the jingling of the bells in her cap: 'Yes' and 'No' at anybody's command, in and out of season.

Thank you, Charles, for your letter! I was beginning to think my invitation to Dayton inexplicable, when that letter arrived. I cannot but deem it an unworthy baseness to entrap a girl to study her without a warning to her. I went up to my room after I had read it, and wrote in reply till the breakfast-bell rang. I resumed my occupation an hour later, and wrote till one o'clock. In all, fifteen pages of writing, which I carefully folded and addressed to Charles; sealed the envelope, stamped it, and destroyed it. I went to bed. 'No, I won't ride out today, I have a headache!' I repeated this about half-a-dozen times to nobody's knocking on the door, and when at last somebody knocked I tried to repeat it once, but having the message that Mr. Pollingray particularly wished to have my company in a ride, I rose submissively and cried. This humiliation made my temper ferocious. Mr. Pollingray observed my face, and put it down in his notebook. 'A savage disposition,' or, no, 'An untamed little rebel'; for he has hopes of me. He had the cruelty to say so.

'What I am, I shall remain,' said I.

He informed me that it was perfectly natural for me to think it; and on my replying that persons ought to know themselves best: 'At my age, perhaps,' he said, and added, 'I cannot speak very confidently of my knowledge of myself.'

'Then you make us out to be nothing better than puppets, Mr. Pollingray.'

'If we have missed an early apprenticeship to the habit of self-command, ma filleule.'

'Merci, mon parrain.'

He laughed. My French, I suppose.

I determined that, if he wanted to study me, I would help him.

'I can command myself when I choose, but it is only when I choose.'

This seemed to me quite a reasonable speech, until I found him looking for something to follow, in explanation, and on coming to sift my meaning, I saw that it was temper, and getting more angry, continued:

'The sort of young people who have such wonderful command of themselves are not the pleasantest.'

'No,' he said; 'they disappoint us. We expect folly from the young.'

I shut my lips. Prince Leboo knew that he must go, and a good gallop reconciled me to circumstances. Then I was put to jumping little furzes and ditches, which one cannot pretend to do without a fair appearance of gaiety; for, while you are running the risk of a tumble, you are compelled to look cheerful and gay, at least, I am. To fall frowning will never do. I had no fall. My gallant Leboo made my heart leap with love of him, though mill-stones were tied to it. I may be vexed when I begin, but I soon ride out a bad temper. And he is mine! I am certainly inconstant to Charles, for I think of Leboo fifty times more. Besides, there is no engagement as yet between Charles and me. I have first to be approved worthy by Mr. and Miss Pollingray: two pairs of eyes and ears, over which I see a solemnly downy owl sitting, conning their reports of me. It is a very unkind ordeal to subject any inexperienced young woman to. It was harshly conceived and it is being remorselessly executed. I would complain more loudly—in shrieks—if I could say I was unhappy; but every night I look out of my window before going to bed and see the long falls of the infant river through the meadow, and the dark woods seeming to enclose the house from harm: I dream of the old inhabitant, his ancestors, and the numbers and numbers of springs when the wildflowers have flourished in those woods and the nightingales have sung there. And I feel there will never be a home to me like Dayton.

Chapter 5

He

For twenty years of my life I have embraced the phantom of the fairest woman that ever drew breath. I have submitted to her whims, I have worshipped her feet, I have, I believe, strengthened her principle. I have done all in my devotion but adopt her religious faith. And I have, as I trusted some time since, awakened to perceive that those twenty years were a period of mere sentimental pastime, perfectly useless, fruitless, unless, as is possible, it has saved me from other follies. But it was a folly in itself. Can one's nature be too stedfast? The question whether a spice of frivolousness may not be a safeguard has often risen before me. The truth, I must learn to think, is, that my mental power is not the match for my ideal or sentimental apprehension and native tenacity of attachment. I have fallen into one of the pits of a well-meaning but idle man. The world discredits the existence of pure platonism in love. I myself can barely look back on those twenty years of amatory servility with a full comprehension of the part I have been playing in them. And yet I would not willingly forfeit the exalted admiration of Louise for my constancy: as little willingly as I would have imperilled her purity. I cling to the past as to something in which I have deserved well, though I am scarcely satisfied with it. According to our English notions I know my name. English notions, however, are not to be accepted in all matters, any more than the flat declaration of a fact will develop it in all its bearings. When our English society shall have advanced to a high civilization, it will be less expansive in denouncing the higher stupidities. Among us, much of the social judgement of Bodge upon the relations of men to women is the stereotyped opinion of the land. There is the dictum here for a man who adores a woman who is possessed by a husband. If he has long adored her, and known himself to be preferred by her in innocency of heart; if he has solved the problem of being her bosom's lord, without basely seeking to degrade her to being his mistress; the epithets to characterise him in our vernacular will probably be all the less flattering. Politically we are the most self-conscious people upon earth, and socially the frankest animals. The terrorism of our social laws is eminently serviceable, for without it such frank animals as we are might run into bad excesses. I judge rather by the abstract evidence than by the examples our fair matrons give to astounded foreigners when abroad.

Louise writes that her husband is paralysed. The Marquis de Mazardouin is at last tasting of his mortality. I bear in mind the day when he married her. She says that he has taken to priestly counsel, and, like a woman, she praises him for that. It is the one thing which I have not done to please her. She anticipates his decease. Should she be free—what then? My heart does not beat the faster for the thought. There are twenty years upon it, and they make a great load. But I have a desire that she should come over to us. The old folly might rescue me from the new one. Not that I am any further persecuted by the dread that I am in imminent danger here. I have established a proper mastery over my young lady. 'Nous avons change de role'. Alice is subdued; she laughs feebly, is becoming conscious—a fact to be regretted, if I desired to check the creature's growth. There is vast capacity in the girl. She has plainly not centred her affections upon Charles, so that a man's conscience might be at ease if—if he chose to disregard what is due to decency. But, why, when I contest it, do I bow to the world's opinion concerning disparity of years between husband and wife? I know innumerable cases of an old husband making a young wife happy. My friend, Dr. Galliot, married his ward, and he had the best wife of any man of my acquaintance. She has been publishing his learned manuscripts ever since his death. That is an extreme case, for he was forty-five years her senior, and stood bald at the altar. Old General Althorpe married Julia Dahoop, and, but for his preposterous jealousy of her, might be cited in proof that the ordinary reckonings are not to be a yoke on the neck of one who earnestly seeks to spouse a fitting mate, though late in life. But, what are fifty years? They mark the prime of a healthy man's existence. He has by that time seen the world, can decide, and settle, and is virtually more eligible—to use the cant phrase of gossips—than a young man, even for a young girl. And may not some fair and fresh reward be justly claimed as the crown of a virtuous career?

I say all this, yet my real feeling is as if I were bald as Dr. Galliot and jealous as General Althorpe. For, with my thorough knowledge of myself, I, were I like either one of them, should not have offered myself to the mercy of a young woman, or of the world. Nor, as I am and know myself to be, would I offer myself to the mercy of Alice Amble. When my filleule first drove into Dayton she had some singularly audacious ideas of her own. Those vivid young feminine perceptions and untamed imaginations are desperate things to encounter. There is nothing beyond their reach. Our safety from them lies in the fact that they are always seeing too much, and imagining too wildly; so that, with a little help from us, they may be taught to distrust themselves; and when they have once distrusted themselves, we need not afterwards fear them: their supernatural vitality has vanished. I fancy my pretty Alice to be in this state now. She leaves us tomorrow. In the autumn we shall have her with us again, and Louise will scan her compassionately. I desire that they should meet. It will be hardly fair to the English girl, but, if I stand in the gap between them, I shall summon up no small quantity of dormant compatriotic feeling. The contemplation of the contrast, too, may save me from both: like the logic ass with the two trusses of hay on either side of him.

Chapter 6

She

I am at home. There was never anybody who felt so strange in her home. It is not a month since I left my sisters, and I hardly remember that I know them. They all, and even papa, appear to be thinking about such petty things. They complain that I tell them nothing. What have I to tell? My Prince! my own Leboo, if I might lie in the stall with you, then I should feel thoroughly happy! That is, if I could fall asleep. Evelina declares we are not eight miles from Dayton. It seems to me I am eight millions of miles distant, and shall be all my life travelling along a weary road to get there again just for one long sunny day. And it might rain when I got there after all! My trouble nobody knows. Nobody knows a thing!

The night before my departure, Miss Pollingray did me the honour to accompany me up to my bedroom. She spoke to me searchingly about Charles; but she did not demand compromising answers. She is not in favour of early marriages, so she merely wishes to know the footing upon which we stand: that of friends. I assured her we were simply friends. 'It is the firmest basis of an attachment,' she said; and I did not look hurried.

But I gained my end. I led her to talk of the beautiful Marquise. This is the tale. Mr. Pollingray, when a very young man, and comparatively poor, went over to France with good introductions, and there saw and fell in love with Louise de Riverolles. She reciprocated his passion. If he would have consented to abjure his religion and worship with her, Madame de Riverolles, her mother, would have listened to her entreaties. But Gilbert was firm. Mr. Pollingray, I mean, refused to abandon his faith. Her mother, consequently, did not interfere, and Monsieur de Riverolles, her father, gave her to the Marquis de Marzardouin, a roue young nobleman, immensely rich, and shockingly dissipated. And she married him. No, I cannot understand French girls. Do as I will, it is quite incomprehensible to me how Louise, loving another, could suffer herself to be decked out in bridal finery and go to the altar and take the marriage oaths. Not if perdition had threatened would I have submitted. I have a feeling that Mr. Pollingray should have shown at least one year's resentment at such conduct; and yet I admire him for his immediate generous forgiveness of her. It was fatherly. She was married at sixteen. His forgiveness was the fruit of his few years' seniority, said Miss Pollingray, whose opinion of the Marquise I cannot arrive at. At any rate, they have been true and warm friends ever since, constantly together interchangeing visits. That is why Mr. Pollingray has been more French than English for those long years.

Miss Pollingray concluded by asking me what I thought of the story. I said: 'It is very strange French habits are so different from ours. I dare say … I hope …, perhaps … indeed, Mr. Pollingray seems happy now.' Her idea of my wits must be that they are of the schoolgirl order—a perfect receptacle for indefinite impressions.

'Ah!' said she. 'Gilbert has burnt his heart to ashes by this time.'

I slept with that sentence in my brain. In the morning, I rose and dressed, dreaming. As I was turning the handle of my door to go down to breakfast, suddenly I swung round in a fit of tears. It was so piteous to think that he should have waited by her twenty years in a slow anguish, his heart burning out, without a reproach or a complaint. I saw him, I still see him, like a martyr.

'Some people,' Miss Pollingray said, 'permitted themselves to think evil of my brother's assiduous devotion to a married woman. There is not a spot on his character, or on that of the person whom Gilbert loved.'

I would believe it in the teeth of calumny. I would cling to my belief in him if I were drowning.

I consider that those twenty years are just nothing, if he chooses to have them so. He has lived embalmed in a saintly affection. No wonder he considers himself still youthful. He is entitled to feel that his future is before him.

No amount of sponging would get the stains away from my horrid red eyelids. I slunk into my seat at the breakfast-table, not knowing that one of the maids had dropped a letter from Charles into my hand, and that I had opened it and was holding it open. The letter, as I found afterwards, told me that Charles has received an order from his uncle to go over to Mr. Pollingray's estate in Dauphiny on business. I am not sorry that they should have supposed I was silly enough to cry at the thought of Charles's crossing the Channel. They did imagine it, I know; for by and by Miss Pollingray whispered: 'Les absents n'auront pas tort, cette fois, n'est-ce-pas? 'And Mr. Pollingray was cruelly gentle: an air of 'I would not intrude on such emotions'; and I heightened their delusions as much as I could: there was no other way of accounting for my pantomime face. Why should he fancy I suffered so terribly? He talked with an excited cheerfulness meant to relieve me, of course, but there was no justification for his deeming me a love-sick kind of woe-begone ballad girl. It caused him likewise to adopt a manner—what to call it, I cannot think: tender respect, frigid regard, anything that accompanies and belongs to the pressure of your hand with the finger-tips. He said goodbye so tenderly that I would have kissed his sleeve. The effort to restrain myself made me like an icicle. Oh! adieu, mon parrain!

Printed in Great Britain
by Amazon

27530812R00030